Your Needs are Special Too...

a salutary for Siblings of Special Needs kids

a book and workbook

written by Charla Cottom Booth
educator and autism mom

...for all the sisters and brothers of special needs kids

...to remind you that you are special too

for Marina, Melissa, Marcus, Maliya, Makenzie, Malani and Mason

...I love you

Your Needs are Special Too...

a salutary for Siblings of Special Needs kids

Table of Contents

Go Away

The ink flowed smoothly from the purple gel pen onto the unlocked pages of the journal. Pent up feelings that had no other way to escape tumbled onto today's tirade,

> "Please somebody make it stop.
>
> Make it go away.
>
> I swear I'm going to kill myself if I
>
> Have to hear this one more day!!"

Well... okay. Maybe not kill myself, she thought, *maybe that is a little dramatic...*

"Summer," she heard her mother call, "Did you fix your brother lunch today?"

"Seriously," Summer wanted to respond, "I am NOT my brother's keeper." But instead all she could manage was a weak, "No. I must have forgot. Again."

"Honey," her mom said plopping down next to her on the bed, "I know this is hard for you. Having a little brother who is autistic and ODD - "

"But mom!" Summer interrupted, "He's so embarrassing. And he hurts me. He always hurts me..."

Robert was only ten but his mood swings were unpredictable and often escalated into Tourette-like cursing tirades and things being thrown her way.

Once he had hurled an ice bucket down the stairs striking her in the face and nearly breaking her nose.

"He doesn't mean to."

Summer could hear the pain and defeat in her mother's voice. She knew how hard her mother had to work since Jeffrey gave up on trying to make them a normal family. He too had grown tired of how they could never go anywhere or do anything without Robert causing a scene.

"I know mom," Summer whispered softly, "I'll try to do better. I know if I don't feed him he won't eat on his own."

"Thank you honey," her mom replied lightly kissing her forehead and giving her hand a squeeze.

Summer looked up into her mother's eyes. They were sympathetic... loving. Summer flung her arms around her mother and gratefully laid her head on her mother's shoulder relishing the moment, but the rare tender exchange was abruptly aborted by what sounded like a chair being hurled against a wall followed by the loud pounding of fists beating against a hollow door.

"Damn it woman! Where's my dinner!"

Summer's mom rushed from the room to try to calm down the explosive rage before it could build. Summer wished she could help but she knew her presence would just make Robert more agitated. She reached for her journal and sighed. *I wish he would just go away.*

Jeffrey had given her the journal saying it might help her get through the bad times if she wrote her feelings down instead of having to keep them bottled up inside.

Well, she thought, *he should've taken his own advice and gotten a journal too because in less than a year he had given up and now he was the one who was gone.*

Surprisingly Summer's mom reappeared in the doorway with a huge grin on her face. What should have been a prophesy of good things to come leered before Summer as a sign of impending dread.

"Summer," her mom began, "I've got a great idea!" was what she said. But Summer only heard, "This is going to be another terrible mess come on and help me make it."

"I was thinking we'd go and get ice cream. Wouldn't that be fun?"

Surely she didn't mean the three of them. It was Friday night. All the kids from Riverside High would be out enjoying these last few warm nights of autumn. The ones she was cool with at her new school didn't know about Robert yet and she wanted to keep it that way.

"Honey, you could wear that new pink jacket I got you," her mom gushed.

"I'm sure other kids would be at the mall. I'd bet you'd make some friends."

Summer thought back to the last time they had taken her brother on an outing. It had only been to the grocery store, but Robert was so overstimulated by all the different smells he'd had a huge meltdown right in the middle of aisle four screaming about being attacked by giant spiders. Not a scene she wanted to be a part of again. Ever.

"It's not a good time mom," Summer lied, "There's a movie I've been waiting weeks to see and it's finally coming on tonight. But you should go and take Robert. He'd have a much better time if I wasn't there dividing your attention. You know how much he loves to be alone with you."

"I hate to admit it but you're probably right," her mother sighed. "I'll bring you something back. Something special."

In the end Robert wouldn't go either so mom went alone promising to bring them both back a treat. Summer dozed off as she restarted the Netflix movie she'd already seen a dozen times.

"Summer," mom's voice sounded odd, "Where's Robert? I can't find him. He's gone."

Summer sat upright on the bed. She'd never heard her mom sound so scared.

"I don't know. I was sleep."

"Damn." Summer's mother never cursed. This was going to be another night for the books. She watched helplessly as her mother dissolved into tears and ran from the house.

"Damn," Summer whispered, "Now I have to go look too."

Day became dusk and night was falling fast. Her cell phone lit up again. "No mom," she answered for the eleventh time, "Not yet."

Where is this stupid boy? she wondered.

Summer leaned against the light post on the corner. She thought back to all the times her life had been forced to revolve around her brother. How he had ruined her birthday Tea Party when she was twelve. Her mother had gone shopping and bought long fancy dresses from all the thrift stores in town so they could look like princesses. But Robert, agitated by the noise, had cursed them all like a drunken sailor.

She remembered her mom's beautiful wedding just last year and how Robert had started yelling about the lights being too bright in the church right in the middle of the vows. Jeffrey had moved them here this past summer to try to give everybody a chance at a fresh new start. But Robert had made that poor man's life a living hell. Even though Jeffrey had tried to be a good father Robert refused to share their mother with anyone else.

● ● ●

Suddenly she knew. Robert loved to fish. It was one of the few things he had enjoyed with Jeff. Robert loved to sit at the pond a few blocks away and watch the fish nibble at his bobber.

Summer ran towards the park. It was getting colder and the wind stung her face. A few drops of rain struck her cheek. *Seriously,* she thought, *could this night get any worse?* And then she saw him. Curled up in a ball sobbing. He was scared but she was too mad to notice. Or to care.

"Dammit Robert! I'm sick of having to take care of you! Get up this instant and come home! Mom is tired of looking for you and I'm just sick of you period!" The words she'd been wanting to say just poured off the pages and out of her mouth. She couldn't stop them. They fell like the rain.

But Robert didn't move. He just cried. And for the first time in a long time Summer's heart was touched. She looked down at the helpless little ball and she remembered how happy and proud she had felt to be a big sister. His big sister.

She remembered how fiercely she had protected him because mom told her he was different and special and would always need her. And so, for the first time in… maybe ever Summer saw Robert for the poor little tortured soul he was. She realized the private hell that he was living in each day. She remembered that she had forgotten to love him.

Robert lifted his head and she saw the desperation in his eyes. *Oh, my God,* Summer thought, *does he want me to make him feel safe?*

"The spiders were chasing me…" Robert sputtered.

Kneeling beside him she whispered, "I made the spiders go away. You're safe now. Come on baby. Let's go home."

And then he hugged her… and she hugged him back. He was her little brother again. That sweet golden-haired little boy with the crooked smile and funny laugh. And then it was over.

"Robert!" She heard her mother exclaim.

Pushing her abruptly to the ground Robert jumped up and ran happily calling "Mommy!"

It was as if the moment had never happened. In a single second everything had returned to normal and Robert was oblivious to her presence.

He would probably never even remember this experience. But she would. She would remember this moment. She would remember the innocence and fear intertwined in his eyes. And she vowed that next time she would try harder. Maybe just a little harder. But she would try.

Go Away: An Exclusive Short Story
This article was featured in Autism Parenting Magazine
Issue 66 – Finding Calm and Balance
December 19, 2017

WORKSHEET #1

1. Have you ever felt embarrassed by your sibling? If so, share the worst situation. What happened? What did they do?

   _____

   _____

   _____

   _____

2. Why were you embarrassed? or If not: How did you handle the potentially embarrassing situation?

   _____

   _____

   _____

3. What do you wish you or the adult in charge had done differently to manage the situation?

   _____

   _____

   _____

4. Do you think the outcome would have been different? If so, how?

   _____

   _____

5. Has your sibling ever run away or physically hurt themselves? If so, what happened?

_____

_____

_____

_____

_____

6. Have you ever had the responsibility of feeding or providing for your sibling? _____ If so, what were you expected to do?

_____

_____

_____

_____

7. How do you feel about the responsibilities you have caring for your sibling?

_____

_____

_____

_____

_____

8. Have you ever wished your sibling would just go away?
   If so, when? Why?

   _____

   _____

   If you have ever felt this way...
   Did it make you feel guilty or sad? Why? or Why not?

   _____

   _____

   _____

   _____

9. What do you think you would do if your sibling was missing?

   _____

   _____

   _____

   _____

   _____

   _____

   _____

   _____

Sister, Sister

Then...

Rachel Leigh Mason had a mind of her own. While everyone else was planning and getting ready to welcome the new Fourth of July addition to the family, Rachel decided April would be a much better month to be born. And so, it began...

Haley didn't understand the big deal. And she didn't care. Her baby sister was finally here and that meant she was going to be a sister. A big sister. Well... she would be... as soon as Rachel was released from NICU. In the meantime, Haley made sure to watch her favorite episode of Dora every day. The one about being a big sister. Her mom had recorded it on the DVR and even though she was only three Haley knew how to replay it over and over on the cable box in the den. Seven long weeks later her little sister finally came home.

As weeks became months and the months became years Haley's fascination with her little sister grew. Haley never quite understood what it meant to miss milestones and projections where Rachel was concerned. It didn't bother her that her little sister never talked and barely cried. In fact, Rachel didn't really like to play and never wanted to be touched or held but she grinned a lot when Haley sang to her or danced her happy dance.

Every evening when dad came home, he would ask Haley about her day and she would always include what she had done to make her sister smile. No matter what difficulties her day had brought her, just seeing Rachel brought her joy.

As the years went by Haley started taking real dance classes. But Rachel never did. So, Haley would practice in front of Rachel knowing it  would make her smile. Then Haley became a cheerleader. But Rachel never did. So, Haley would practice her cheers in front of Rachel and try to get her to imitate the moves. Rachel never did but Haley loved to try. Then Haley became the best speller at her school, but Rachel didn't even go to school. Well... not really. She went to a special school – an ABA facility that would teach her how to be better at managing life skills and how to cope with surviving the overwhelming obstacles of getting through each day.

Now....

The summer Haley turned thirteen she asked her parents for a party. A real birthday party with dress-up clothes and church shoes. Strawberry frappé and a full sheet cake to be devoured at home after a real grown up dinner at Giovanni's – the most authentic Italian restaurant in town.

Dad was worried for Haley's sake, but agreed and made the plans.

In perfect weather the entire family in their fanciest attire piled into the old minivan and headed in to town. When they arrived, there was a waiting host of family and friends seated at a long table along a wall of tall dimly-lit windows. The waiter appeared, and everyone excitedly ordered their favorite dish. When he got to Rachel who was seated between mom and me playing with a long piece of purple string my mother smiled sweetly and asked if he would bring her plain spaghetti and a few meatballs but on separate saucers to they wouldn't touch. The waiter looked curiously at mom as if trying to decide whether she was from another galaxy or just another planet then quickly moved on to inquire what she wanted for herself. The evening was perfect. The restaurant was perfect. In fact, everything was going perfectly. And then the food arrived.

The moment the waiter sat Rachel's little plates onto the table I knew things were about to change. The spaghetti was covered in bright red sauce that looked like zombie blood. It dripped off every strand, pooling near the edge and threatening to trickle over the side if anyone so much as breathed. And the meatballs. They weren't just big they were huge. Gargantuan. Prickling with pieces of green onion and smelling like vampire garlic. Then someone sneezed. And the table vibrated. Just a little. And one giant meatball shifted to the edge of its saucer touching the lava bleeding over the edge of the too near little plate. Rachel gasped. The entire table fell silent. Waiting.

Well, we sure didn't have to wait long because Rachel let out a shriek that silenced the entire room full of fancy bourgeois diners. Wide eyes and even wider open mouths glared in our direction.

Mom jumped up handing the offending dishes to the startled waiter and shouted something to dad while frantically pointing out of the nearest velvet-draped window.

Dad jumped up knocking over his water and flooding his ravioli into a sloppy soupy mess.

My little cousin Albert started to cry, and Aunt Edna looked like a circus clown scurrying around to his side of the table throwing her arms around his shoulders and almost strangling him with her more than ample bosom hoping to shush him before the other guests got mad.

Mom calmly handed Rachel back her fallen string and smoothed a few stray hairs from my sister's sweating brow. Rachel started rocking and became immersed in twirling the string from one finger to the next. Crisis averted. Well… at least over.

Dad ran back in clutching something to his chest followed by a stout curly haired maître d' trying to snatch the white paper bag adorned with the huge golden M on the front from dad's hands.

Uncle Clarence stood up abruptly blocking his path and politely offered, "If you want your other guests to enjoy their meal, you'd better let that little girl have this one."

The server looked over at Rachel now quietly swaying from side to side happily munching a plain chicken nugget. Throwing up his hands in an overly dramatic fashion he mumbled something that sounded a little profane under his breath and walked hurriedly back towards the kitchen.

Dad came around and hugged my shoulders muttering an apology about ruining my dinner. I hugged him back and whispered in his ear that everything was fine. I was my sister's sister and as long as she was happy, I was happy too.

Dad pulled away and looked first into my eyes and then into my soul. He saw the unconditional love I have always had for Rachel and he saw my love for him.

Mom gave his shoulder a little squeeze and kissed me on the cheek. Rachel looked up and smiled at me and all was well with the world.

WORKSHEET #2

1. Are you the older or the younger sibling?

   _____

2. If older, do you remember anticipating your sibling being born? If younger, do you remember your early childhood with your sibling?

   _____

   _____

3. What is one memory that stands out to you from your childhood that involved your sister or brother in which your goal was to make them happy.

   _____

   _____

   _____

   _____

   _____

4. Does your sibling have a food they enjoy?

   _____

   Do they have foods they refuse to eat?

   _____

   _____

5. What happens when they are presented with foods they hate?

_____

_____

_____

_____

6. How does their reaction to undesired foods make you feel?

_____

_____

_____

7. Has your sibling ever prevented you from going to a restaurant or place you wanted to eat in? If yes, how did that make you feel?

_____

_____

If not, has dining out in public restaurants always been a good choice?

_____

_____

_____

8. Have you ever felt that if your parent(s) made different choices with your sibling when they were still little, they would have better reactions when presented with more varieties of food?

_____

_____

_____

_____

9. Have you ever done anything to help or change their negative reaction just because you wanted them to be happy?

_____

_____

_____

_____

10. Did doing so make you feel happy? How did it make you feel?

_____

_____

_____

If you have not, why not?

_____

_____

SHUT UP

Today I hit my brother. Just punched him right in the face. And it was the best feeling in the world.

I don't know how long I've been wanting to do that. Waiting to do that. I can't even remember when it first occurred to me that I ought to do it. Needed to do it ...but it was always there. Lurking in the back of my mind. Peeking out into my now and rearing its ugly head in the mist of my beautiful daydreams. Silently urgently egging me on. Cheering. For me. Championing my successful achievement long before the dastardly deed was done ...day after day, week after week, month after month. Maybe even years. Whispering to me how vindicated I would be. How good I would feel to finally shut up that sink hole orifice of a mouth just once stopping that constant stream of incessant babble.

And you know what? My subconscious was right...

It worked.

For that one glorious moment in time he finally shut up.

One simple jab was all it took to change his behavior.

One simple jab was all it took to change all our lives...

Forever.

At that second, I felt good. No, I felt great. All of the toys I'd had to give up when I clearly didn't want to share. All of the meals I never got to eat because Benny couldn't have food from there. All of the shows I had to turn off because the noise from the set was hurting his ears. All of the places I never got to go because he would be overstimulated or devastated or there was just no one available to watch him.

Everything I've ever missed out on was made okay with one quick punch.

I needed to get him back and finally had the courage to do it. Without even planning it I had achieved the most momentous accomplishment of my life and quite possibly the most unforgivable.

No one is ever really prepared for death. It is complete. It changes everything. Although everything and everyone else in life continue on something is always just a little different.

And so it was for me. No. No one died. I didn't kill him I just smacked him and it wasn't even really that hard.

But the aftermath was something I had never truly considered in my selfish quest for revenge.

I was also not prepared for Benny's reaction.

The precious moment of silence was followed by what I can only describe as the most hideous wailing moan I've ever heard. He was clutching his face with his hands and falling backwards to his knees.

 It was like the matrix. That slow motion arching whirling spin spiraling steadily sluggishly listlessly downwards with the uttermost certainty of no possibility for return.

Then he curled up in a little ball, fetal like on the carpet rocking meticulously from side to side grasping his cheeks and softly wailing not comprehending the severity of his pain but completely understanding that I had caused it.

My father stood frozen in the doorway. Appalled at the actuality that it had finally come to this. Unsure of which of us to address first but opting for the obvious and rushing to Benny's side trying to calm him with his words because only mother was allowed to touch.

And then mom appeared. Right on cue.

Hovering in the doorway calculating all the possible scenarios and focusing on my Rocky like stance

appropriately screaming –

"Kendall what have you done?"

And that's when it all died.

Trust was the first to go. It would be weeks almost a month before I could go anywhere near Benny without him flinching and recoiling from what could be another hurt.

It would be even longer before my parents felt comfortable leaving us alone in the house and sometimes even the room.

But I realized almost instantly what I had done. I recognized my courage as cowardice. Seeking vengeance for years of disappointment and bitterness instead of insisting my parents consider and deal with my feelings too.

Benny couldn't help how he was. He couldn't change who he was. For all I know he was more miserable living as him than I was living with him. But before that point it was an angle I had never considered. A reality that not ever had been made real.

And even though I said I was sorry. And even though my parents knew it was true we all knew I could never take it back. Especially Benny who forgave me long before he probably should have and chose to continue to love me anyway.

Don't get me wrong. I still get irritated by Benny's interminable chatter but now I try to find a way to cope. My parents are even trying to make an effort to acknowledge how his needs are affecting mine.

And as much as I wish sometimes he would just shut up – I only take matters in to my own hands when I can offer a way to help – not hurt.

WORKSHEET #3

1. Have you ever wanted to hurt your sibling in any way?

_____

_____

2. Have you ever physically hurt or touched your sibling in an inappropriate manner? If so, what happened?

_____

_____

_____

   How did that make you feel?

_____

_____

_____

3. Did your parent(s) know? _____
   If so, who? What was their reaction?

_____

_____

_____

_____

4. If not, do you think you should talk to your parent(s) about it? Why or why not?

_____

_____

_____

_____

5. Are you able to talk with your sibling about how you feel towards them or about your relationship? _____

If yes, does talking help? If no, how frustrating is this for you?

_____

_____

_____

_____

6. Who do you talk to about your feelings towards your sibling?

_____

_____

_____

7. Why do you feel you can trust them with your feelings?

_____

_____

Breathe

The finish line was in sight. I could see the head judge and the recorder moving into place and positioning the video camera just in case the winner wasn't clearly definitive. I could feel Jeremy Strickland coming up on my left and from the corner of my right eye I could see Lathan O'Brien pressing forward and moving right up alongside my shoulder. I pumped harder with my arms. My legs were on fire. At any second my chest was going to explode. Breathe. I needed to breathe. Flaring my nostrils, I sucked inward fast and deep and my body responded instantly. I remembered my coach playfully teasing and telling me I could "make the jump to light speed." And I had.

Feeling a fresh burst of energy, I raced harder and was able to move two paces ahead leaving Jeremy and Lathan to fight for the silver. And then it was over. I had done it. I was the fastest middle school runner in the whole city. I had qualified for the state meet. I was a champion. A hero. The best.

My eyes searched through the crowd. My dad had come from his new home in Scranton just to see me race. I knew he would be proud. He was the reason I started running. He... and Mason.

The ceremony began. I stepped up on the highest block smiling and waving as my name was called. I leaned forward bending from the waist as the shiny gold medal dangling on a bright blue ribbon with tiny white stars was placed over my head. I stood. The crowd cheered. I scanned their faces. Where was he?

The rest of the ceremony was a blur.

Awkwardly I moved down from the podium almost tripping over myself. Other parents were leading their kids towards the school locker room to get their stuff then on to their cars to go home.

"Great job Malik." I heard my coach say proudly as he patted me on the back. "Now everybody knows what I already knew. You are officially the fastest kid in Ohio!" I nodded and grinned stupidly barely hearing his praise. *Where was my dad?*

And then I saw him. And my mom. And a small crowd of about six or seven people smirking, and leering, and recording the scene. A horn blew and Mason who had almost been convinced to come out of the busy road was frightened and took off running into the moving traffic. Again. I yelled at dad not to chase him. I knew Mason's MO. The paranoia of being pursued would only make him run faster. And further.

Mom saw me and waved me over. She was crying. Instantly I was sorry for having insisted on calling dad and asking him to come. I knew seeing him would be hard on her. But I wanted him here. Needed him here. Needed to know he was here just for me.

This time I wanted to be the one who was special. I wanted to be the center of attention. Today I wanted to be the son they thought about first.

Another horn blew thrusting me back to reality. I quickly assessed the situation. It was almost funny in a pitiful sort of way. Mason and dad going round and round darting and dodging through the slowly moving cars on our side of the busy street was sadly hilarious. Then just as dad was about to grab him Mason jumped and rolled over the hood of a shiny red sports car and ran a little further down the road. Dad started to pursue him again, but the driver of the Corvette had jumped out of the car and held dad by the arm yelling at him and pointing at the shiny unblemished hood.

I wanted to ask mom if they had seen me win. Heck, I wanted to ask her if they'd even seen the race. If dad had finally been able to feel proud of at least one of his sons.

I glanced again at mom clutching Madalyn to her chest. She looked helpless and scared. Maddy started to cry too.

"Breathe" I heard myself telling her as I swept a tear from her soft little cheek, "I'll get him."

I started running through the grassy edge of the field which intersected with the road up ahead. I knew it was important that Mason not see me approach. My mind wandered again. It was utterly ironic for dad to be in this situation.

When Mason was little he would cry. A lot. And for no apparent reason. As he got older his cries would often turn to screeches. High pitched and constant. It could go on for hours. Mom had just given birth to Maddy and was often preoccupied with a fussy colicky premature infant who also needed special care.

Once he came home in the evenings dad spent the most time with Mason, but dad's job was stressful and he came home mentally drained.

One day dad couldn't take it anymore. Said he felt like a caged animal always cooped up in the house. He dressed Mason and I warmly, put on our sneakers, and told mom he was taking us outside. That day I learned to jog. The next week we started to run. Mason loved it. I don't know if it was the wind on his face or the trees blurring as we sped by but something in him was set free when we ran and our outings became longer and faster.

Then dad's company closed.

Mason and Maddy were both more expensive than normal kids and a savings account was a luxury that neither of my parents had. Without a job dad was quickly becoming short tempered and financially frustrated. He and mom started to argue. A lot.

One day things were thrown and the next day dad left. I was never sure who had thrown what at whom and I guess in the long run it didn't really matter cause either way dad was gone.

• • •

I cut over towards the curve of the road and I could see Mason weaving through the traffic. I dashed into the slowly moving cars just ahead of him and without making eye contact started to jog right down the yellow line in the middle of the road. A slow but steady pace. Praying.

And then he was there. Beside me. Matching my stride. I looked over at him and smiled. He smiled back. We ran like that side by side for about a mile. The road was coming to a fork.

I yelled "Come on" and took off running. The pavement veered slightly onto a small service road and we took it. And then we were running full out and free in the wind. Mason leading the way.

Unaccustomed to the uneven terrain I tripped and stumbled falling to the soft grass beneath my feet. I lay there alone for a moment trying to figure out my next move.

And then he was there. Mason had come back to see if I was alright.

I took the emergency cellphone from the little pack he wore fastened securely around his waist. Reassuring mom I told her where we were and that we were both okay.

Mason sat on the grass beside me. Tired from the run and exhausted from the ordeal. He patted my leg as if it were he who was comforting and taking care of me. Then he asked me if I was hurt and apologized for beating me. I looked in his eyes. He was sad that he had outrun me. I laughed and remembered how much I loved my big brother.

Smiling again I deftly removed the medal from my neck and placed it over his head. "It's okay," I told him, "Congratulations for winning." He laid his head on my shoulder as he fingered the glistening coin. The shiny gold fell gently against his panting chest.

"Breathe," I whispered, "everything is going to be okay...".

He smiled and I felt him let out a long sigh of relief.

Hearing the car we looked up as mom jumped out and ran over to where we sat. Dad followed with Maddy looking equally concerned.

"Look!" Mason exclaimed. "I won!"

"Malik!" Mom whispered, "You won?"

Dad looked sheepishly at the ground clearly troubled for having missed my race.

"I'm sorry son," he began, "I know this was your special day. I'm so proud of you. You are very special to me... and your mother."

"And me too," Maddy chimed in throwing her chubby little arms around my neck.

And Mason laughed throwing his face to the air the sounds coming like screeching joy. It was horrible and beautifully contagious all at the same time. My parents were frozen neither wanting to say or do the wrong thing and spoil the moment.

"Breathe" I told them.

And they did. And we all laughed. That moment became as golden as that medal. And as we sat there on the side of the road laughing with our faces to the wind, I knew that in our own way each of us was special. We were all winners that day.

WORKSHEET #4

1. Have you ever felt like your accomplishments did not get the recognition they deserved from members of your family?

_____

_____

_____

2. Has your sibling's condition caused attention to be taken away from you?

_____

_____

_____

3. Have you talked to your parents about this? How did that go?

_____

_____

_____

4. Does your sibling have a talent the world may never see?

_____

_____

5. Are there some fun things that you can do with your sibling?

_____

_____

6. Are there fun things that your whole family enjoys together?

_____

_____

7. Has your sibling ever been in a situation that made you afraid for their safety? If so, what happened? what did you or your parents do?

_____

_____

_____

_____

_____

8. How do you feel when situations occur that are out of your control?

_____

_____

_____

_____

_____

Tripping

"I'm not going and you can't make me."

Not now. Not five minutes before we have to be in the car.

"Delia, please... please do this for mommy."

"I'm not going and you can't make me!"

As usual my big sister was right. Maybe four years and a hundred pounds ago mom could've. But not now. Not anymore.

We'd been planning this trip for months. Mom had seen to every detail. She had painstakingly gone over every aspect with Delia at least once a day every day for the past week. Yesterday everything was fine and Delia, though never one to show excitement, seemed agreeable to the plan. She had even let mom pack her suitcase in her room – a space that is normally off limits to all of us.

My mind was racing. I had to do something. This was the closest we had been to taking a real vacation in years. Who knows when mom would get up the courage to try to do this again. I couldn't wait. I had to do that something now. I had to say something to help. I mean, it was pretty much now or never. Leveling my voice and trying to sound as casual as possible I mentioned,

"Well I'm going to get a cup of coffee. Dee, do you want some?"

Mom looked at me appreciatively.

This distraction was just what we needed.

Moments into sipping the steaming hot liquid Delia began to calm down. It was funny how this worked. You know. The caffeine that makes everyone else so wide awake, hype and jittery has just the opposite effect on most ADHD kids... That negative plus a negative equal a positive outcome. It's not math – it's coffee but it works just the same. And thankfully even though mine was so watered down it was practically just brown-stained water Delia's was a double shot of expresso and by the time mom said -

"Let's go" Delia headed happily back to the car.

"Hey Dee, want a thermos to go?"

"Kathleen!"

"Okay. Sorry mom. Never mind Dee, let's go."

Traffic was light and uneventful as we quickly made our way out of the familiar neighborhood and onto the open highway. We were actually doing it this time. We were really going to make it to Michigan to visit Aunt Jillian. I hadn't seen her in over a year. She was mom's older sister and gave the best hugs in the world. Something I felt I hadn't had since the last time she came to visit.

The lurching of the car brought me quickly out of my euphoric daydream

 and into the harsh realities of the ride. Traffic had practically stopped. We weren't moving. *What had happened? When did it get so heavy?*

"Mom…" I asked cautiously not wanting to upset the pleasant climate of the car.

"It's fine," she answered calmly, "Looks like a minor accident up ahead but I'm sure it'll be cleared away soon." Relieved I closed my eyes and slipped easily back into my happy thoughts.

Well. Mom was wrong. It wasn't minor and we weren't moving. Even with the windows rolled completely down the heat from the rising sun was making life in the backseat pretty uncomfortable. And I wasn't the only one who noticed.

"Mom, I'm hot. I want to go home!"

I kept my eyes shut tight. Afraid to move. I may even have stopped breathing. I was so afraid to give Delia any reason to be more upset.

Blessedly the heavens must have heard my silent prayers because traffic began to roll forward and our car was finally able to move.

Within minutes we were out on the open road mom's hair lifting like angel wings behind her as the coolness of the gentle breeze blew softly into the back seat with us. We rode for almost an hour like this. I was dozing mom was humming, and Aunt Jillian was getting closer with every mile. Mom pulled the car into a Burger Spot parking lot and offered cool drinks

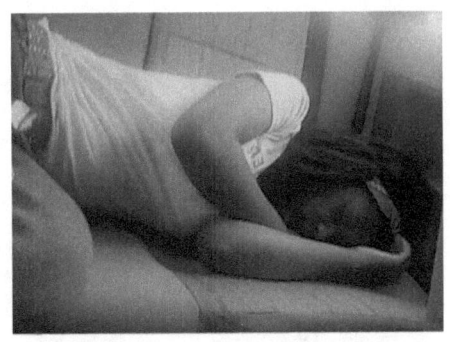

and a potty break. Even though I didn't have to go I took Delia. Better safe than sorry. I looked around for paper towels but to my chagrin saw only those incredibly loud automatic hand dryers that most SPD kids absolutely hate. Today would be no exception.

I looked at Delia's face as she watched the lady at the sink wash her hands. I saw Dee squint as the lady moved towards the contraption that was sure to spoil an otherwise insignificant moment. And I saw Delia cover her ears with her hands as her eyes grew wide already hating the impending burst of air and noise. I chose what I thought was the lesser of two evils and forcibly pushed Delia out of the restroom and into the lobby without giving her a chance to wash her own hands. Apparently, an equivalent error in judgement as Delia angrily announced to the entire diner that I had not let her do so.

Mom rushed over and shoved two cups into my hands while steering Dee back into the Ladies Room in one swift smooth move. I sat at a nearby table and waited for the fallout.

None came. Delia emerged with a smile on her face, took the nearest cup and proceeded to enjoy the cool pink lemonade as it pulsed upwards through her straw. I looked at mom who was beaming that triumphant mom-saved-the-day smile that she wears when she somehow manages to diffuse that ticking time-bomb I call my sister.

"Look. Napkins!" Dee announced proudly waving a handful and stuffing them into a rear pocket. We chuckled and relaxed.

The day had been saved again.

Back in the car things were calm. Traffic had grown a little heavier, but we were less than an hour away from the delicious smells and warm hugs. I closed my eyes once more. I didn't take naps often but the thought of staying up late cooking and helping Aunt Jill inspired me to want to be rested and ready. Less than two minutes into la-la-land all that changed... and not for the better.

With no indicators, no signs, no warning and no apparent trigger Delia was in a rage. Why? Had the batteries died in her headphones? Had the tablet lost the wi-fi hotspot connection from mom's phone? Did the coffee suddenly wear off? What???

I didn't know then and don't understand now. What I do know was that Delia was out-of-control and this time I wasn't able to calm her down. She was yelling. Arms flailing. She was tugging at her seatbelt screaming at mom to stop the car so she could get out.

The belt unbuckled and all hell broke loose.

Mom was swerving in traffic trying to look back over her shoulder and talk Delia down. But Dee wasn't having it. Then I made the mistake of moving. Of asking her to calm down.

Everybody knows that the worst thing you can do to an ODDer when they are having a meltdown is to give them a verbal command. There is no way they can process it and that just makes things worse. They need written options and directives. But I didn't have a worksheet and Delia didn't have control. She was mad. She was mad at the world and she took it out on me.

Twisting in her seat she began kicking me unmercifully... my thighs, my arms, even my face became the receiver of her angst. She was kicking, and I was screaming – begging mom to pullover and stop. And there was mom baby talking Delia in that calm voice – politely asking -

"Please don't kick your sister."

Her words fell on deaf ears as Delia kicked harder. Below the pretty blue edge of my shorts my thigh was turning a hideous shade of deep purple. My upper arm was throbbing and a final "whack" from the leather sole of her sandal promised to leave me with yet another black eye.

"Dee, Stop!" I screamed again. "Mom, help!"

But mom kept driving and kept talking to Delia asking her to calm down.

Promising her all kinds of stupid stuff if she'd just "Be good."

 In the end – I don't know if it was lucidity or sheer exhaustion, but Delia began to calm down. She cried softly and curled away from me into the door on her side. Mom was explaining to me how she couldn't stop the car. Delia was prone to run and when crazed had no real fear or concern for the dangers of moving traffic or the waters of the lake just off the side of the road.

I heard mom. I heard every word and maybe somewhere, somehow, someday these facts would matter.

But right now.

Right now,

I loathed them both.

Delia for hurting me

– again.

And mom for letting her

– again.

The pain in my heart a thousand times worse than the pain ripping through my jaw and upwards across the right side of my face.

The pain in knowing that once again I had been beaten, and abused, and hurt and once again my mother had let it happen...

Once again she had chosen Delia over me.

I hadn't even noticed that the car had stopped, and Delia was happily playing with Mr. Bentley the family dog. Mom was smiling and laughing with Uncle Mike as they pulled our luggage from the trunk. And then she was there. Aunt Jillian on the porch quietly surveying the situation.

Her smile faded when her eyes met my tear-streaked face still pressed against the glass. I lifted my hand to my throbbing cheek. Her eyes grew wide with concern. Mom hugged her briefly as she went into the house holding Delia's hand like a prized possession.

I just watched. Too traumatized to move. Forgotten.

And then she was here – sliding softly into the car seat beside me. She smiled with the curl of her lips, but tears fell from beneath her dark lowered lashes. It was as if she knew. I turned. And there she was. Arms open. Outstretched. Waiting to give me the best hug in the world.

WORKSHEET #5

1. What are the labels that people say your sibling has?

    _____   _____   _____   _____

    Do you understand what the letters mean?

    _____

    _____

    _____

    _____

    Do you understand how this diagnosis contributes to your sibling's actions and behaviors?

    _____

    _____

2. Has your sibling ever physically hurt you in any way? If so, how?

    _____

    _____

    _____

    How did that make you feel?

    _____

    _____

3. Do you feel that your parents protect you and take care of you as much as they do for your sibling?

_____

_____

_____

4. What do you wish your parents knew about how you feel?

_____

_____

_____

_____

_____

5. Do you have someone who you are able to confide in who loves you no matter what? Do they know how you feel?

_____

_____

_____

6. Do you think anyone in your family needs counseling? Explain.

_____

_____

_____

I See You

A woman scolds her young child for taking candy from a box on the shelf. He cries a moment clasping his tiny hands together. Satisfied that he has been adequately admonished his mother turns back to her mission of scanning the remaining items in the now half-empty grocery cart.

The small boy reaches for another candy. He looks up just in time to see my watchful eye spying his act.

Yea, I see you.

Amused, he smiles. I smile back. Without a sound he deftly slips his fingers around the tasty treat and drops it into the diaper bag propped beside him on the front seat of the buggy.

Our eyes return to his mother still busy with her task. He smiles, content with his success. I smile impressed with his calculations. My brother laughed at the entire exchange....

a singular simple reaction that changed both of our lives forever.

"Mom! Mom!" I said excitedly. "Devin laughed at that boy!"

Distractedly my mother turned her gaze to my joviality and gave me a confused look.

Clearly, she did not understand the immensity of this moment.

"Armando, what are you talking about? What boy?"

I pointed excitedly at the adorable toddler sitting in the cart in front of us in the line.

He too was smiling with no hint of the mischievousness he had so recently displayed.

"Okay. That is a cute kid but Devin smiles at everybody so what's the big deal?"

"The deal is..." I began then stopped dead in my tracks.

Should I rat out the poor kid and get him reprimanded yet again for his thievery. Should I try to explain that somehow Devin had not only comprehended what was going on in front of him but responded appropriately. Or should I just keep quiet and hope for another opportunity to witness for myself whether or not Devin had a brain that worked or just imperceivably coincidental timing.

"Well?" she asked impatiently.

Not wanting to make myself look ridiculous I muttered

"Nothing" and "Never mind" and returned my gaze to Devin's.

He was watching the mother buttoning the toddler's sweater. She zipped the diaper bag closed and slung it on her shoulder and lifted the little thief into her arms.

The girl who had bagged her groceries stepped behind the cart and led the way pushing it towards the exit. The little boy glanced back at us smiling triumphantly and Devin smiled again.

Yea, I see you.

I tapped him on the shoulder causing him to turn and look at me. The smile vanished. I pointed to the boy and waved. The jubilant toddler being carried into oblivion waved back. I laughed and looked at Devin. He smiled then laughed again. I was right. He knew.

I began to watch Devin more and more. Really watch him. For the first time I noticed how focused his eyes would be on things happening around him. Sometimes he would still be wearing his normal silly grin or babbling unintelligibly or bouncing off the walls but his eyes… his eyes would be really focused on whatever was happening around him.

I decided to devise a test. Something I could show my parents that would make them believe that Devin was more than the animate object that lived within their walls. That night proved to be perfect.

My parents were in the next room quietly talking with our neighbors from next door. The mole from the woods behind our homes had made his way into both of our front yards. Dad wanted to kill it but the women were pleading their case for a humane trap for the lowly creature. Devin was seated on the floor in front of a kid's channel on the family room TV - a line of cars perfectly framing his sanctum.

I sat beside him placing my hand on his thigh. He seemed not to notice and completely ignored my presence.

A few minutes later I started to cough. Then gasp. I looked at Devin. Nothing. Clutching his thigh as I went down, I pretended to pass out falling limply sideways onto the floor. I waited. Nothing. Good thing I wasn't going to die for real. See, this was why even though I tried I had never really liked him. All that time and all that attention my parents had lavished on him when he was a child – all those moments meant for me that he stole that I could never get back. All the times they treated me like I was second when clearly I should have been first and for what?
Nothing. This kid was going to let me die.

I had just about given up my play when I saw through the sliver of sight between my half-closed lids the look of alarm of Devin's face. *I see you.* He moved. At first, I thought he was smelling me. I held my breath more out of fear of disturbing his study than out of my planned demise. He shook me. Hard. I didn't move. And then he was gone. He had left me alone to die. I don't know what reaction I was expecting but this was an epic fail.

Then I heard them. My parents. Shooing Devin away. He was moaning and from what I could hear pawing dad relentlessly. Then I heard it. Loud and clear. A glass breaking in the doorway then footsteps. Then silence.
It was as if the whole house had died with me. And then they were here. Everyone. Crowding around to see. Calling my name.

Smiling I opened my eyes triumphantly shouting,

"I knew it!" I jumped to my feet.

"I know he understands what's going on." I explained. "I tried to tell you!"

Silence. Again. My parents were aghast.

They must have thought I was crazy.

Then they got it. Devin. I was talking about Devin.

Everyone turned and looked at my little brother sitting silently staring into space. Non-verbal and non-responsive. He looked just the way he always does at any given moment in time.

But this time was different.

They saw him

Yea, really saw him..

And this time we knew that his retreat was temporary.

A place where he lived…

but maybe, just maybe, now that we all knew he could leave…

not the place he would be bound to remain forever.

WORKSHEET #6

1. Do you have a sibling that is non-verbal? _____

   Do you think it is or would be more difficult to have a sibling that doesn't speak?

   _____

   _____

   _____

2. What are some of the challenges that families face who have a non-verbal child?

   _____

   _____

   _____

   _____

3. How would/ does having a non-speaking sibling affect your relationships with friends or other relatives or family members?

   _____

   _____

   _____

   _____

4. Do you believe that not having the ability to speak makes a person less able to understand other things?

_____

_____

_____

5. Should families accept that their special needs child may never speak or should they have hope and try to teach their child to talk?

_____

_____

_____

6. Does your sibling communicate well, or do you believe they know more than they can express?

_____

_____

_____

7. If your sibling has good communication skills do you get to have the conversations with them you would like to have?

_____

_____

When You're Not the one that's Special

Giovanni Carpenter was nobody's fool. He was a streetwise punk of a kid who seemed to take great pleasure in disappointing his parents. Both of them. He was smaller than most of the boys his age and a whole lot

smarter too. He was the type of kid who could be first in just about anything if he wanted to. But he didn't. He was perfectly happy being the kid with the most detentions in the whole school. A feat that he'd also been able to accomplish his two previous years at Edgar Miller Jr. High and one that had left his teachers baffled and stymied. And now nearing the end of his eighth-grade year with only a few months to redeem himself his teachers – and his parents – were left to wonder how he was ever

going to make it through high school.

Everyday was a new adventure. Everyday had the potential to be even more outlandish than the day before. He made sure of that. You see, along with his stubborn arrogant pride and quick wit Giovanni had a quick temper and a slick mouth. His snide sarcastic cynicism kept everyone anticipating and wondering what he would say next while dreading and hoping he wouldn't say anything. Or at least nothing aimed in their direction. Even his teachers knew they were fair game and would often try to pacify or ignore him to avoid becoming the object of his wrath. All of his teachers. Except Dr. Reed. Dr. Reed was old. He had been teaching successfully for over forty years and he was not about to be coerced or distressed by a student's behavior. Not even Giovanni's.

One Friday afternoon Dr. Reed interrupted his students' mid-task and asked them to put their pencils down.

Although he often engaged his classes in moderated discussions and interactive dialogues this diversion from writing time was unprecedented and completely unexpected. It worked. Dr. Reed had succeeded in garnering everyone's attention. Even Giovanni's.

"Next week," Dr. Reed began…. He was smiling. Not that normal pleasant tolerant teacher smile. But a face-splitting, happy grinning love-your-neighbor kind of smile. All teeth.

> *Bad sign* thought Giovanni…
>
> "We're going to be hosting a very special day here in our classroom."
>
> Dr. Reed's smile grew even broader. Gums.
>
> *Real bad…*
>
> "Unbeknownst to you I have contacted all of your guardians and gotten permission to implement this special project." Dr. Reed walked over to a table no one had really noticed before. He removed the cloth uncovering the pile of technology hidden below.

● ● ●

"I wrote a proposal for a classroom grant and we won!"

Silence...

"Do you know what that makes us?" He queried excitedly.

That question seemed a bit too simplistic.

"Uhm... winners?" Asked one student nervously.

"No" said Dr. Reed, "Producers! "

Deafening silence...

"You're going to produce a mini-documentary about your wonderful families which we're all going to watch!"

Dr. Reed went on to explain how the school had petitioned for an opportunity to be a test-pilot center for a new kind of disposable camera that had the ability to record and edit video that was playable through the use of Wi-Fi containing software....

The words just began to run together incoherently for Giovanni. His mind got stuck somewhere between "wonderful" "families" and "watch".

"Gio. Gio?" *Someone was calling his name.* "It's your turn."

Giovanni looked up through a haze of troubled uncertainty to see Dr. Reed standing by the table. In his outstretched hand was a small black rectangular box with what was clearly a lens on the back.

For the first time in a long time Giovanni was visibly shaken. He hesitated, a sense of dread overtaking any attempt at humor or courage.

"Hurry up Giovanni," Carolyn urged, "I want mine and I'm next."

Gathering his swag and regaining his cool Giovanni rose and sauntered to the front of the room. He was just about to make one of his usual un-wise cracks when he saw the paper Dr. Reed held in his other hand. A school contract clearly boasting his father's signature just below the blank space for his own.

Giovanni's heart sank. His parents already knew about the assignment. How was anything he could film over the weekend going to show his family as wonderful?

Trying to steady his trembling hand he signed his name in the space provided agreeing to return the device in excellent condition at the end of the project.

No problem there… he thought to himself… *it won't even get used.*

Spinning around suddenly he swung the camera towards the class.

"Carolyn Patrice Jenkins! Come on down and claim your prize! You are the next contestant on The Price is Write!" He exclaimed waving the signature pencil still in his hand.

"You get it? Write!" he laughed waving the invisible pencil making letter loops in the air. The whole class laughed with him. Even Dr. Reed let out a chuckle. Giovanni let out a sigh of relief. The awkward moment was over and all was right with the world. At least for now.

That afternoon Giovanni sat on the bus contemplating his fate. He would have 48 hours to record all the things and all of the people who left major influences and impressions on his life. His project was to show how these memories are reflected in his daily interactions and personal relationships. He looked at the examples on the directions:

#1. My grandpa played catch with me every day when I was little so now I'm

    a) a catcher on a baseball team with my friends

    b) an avid baseball fan and watch games with my dad

    c) teaching my little brother to play catch

Giovanni's heart stopped again. In fact, this time it jumped up and made a lump in his throat. This was not the only example, but he could just not get past the visualizations this one brought. He would need to capture on film either

- playing a game with his friends

- watching a game with his dad, or

- playing with his little brother

Well none of this was going to happen. He

- didn't have any friends

- never spent any time with his dad

well... he did have a little brother but...

- play with ... not happening.

He knew what he had to do. Giovanni entered the apartment and went straight to his room. Sitting at his little study with the camera hidden safety under his bunk he leaned his forehead as close to the lamp as the dared without burning the skin right off. He sat there for as long as he could bear then yelled for his mom. Seconds later she rushed into his room and hurried over to where he sat curled up moaning on his beanbag chair. Placing her hand on his forehead she rushed right back out to get the thermometer from the room next door. Kyle's room. Of course.

Pulling off his shirtsleeve and muttering her concern she placed the thermometer into the still hairless armpit and proceeded to wait for the beep. Using his manipulative quick wit Giovanni asked for a glass of water. With ice. As she left the room, he called out to his mom to close the door so he would not be disturbed. Not that he ever was.

The second he heard the door latch click into place Giovanni was off the chair and back at the light this time holding the bulged end of the temperature gauge next to the glowing sphere. A moment later he heard 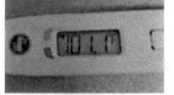 the soft padding of his mother's footsteps in the hall. The door swung open just as he leapt to his place on the chair. 101.1F. Not bad for 60 seconds. Feigning distress at the directive to get in bed until tomorrow Giovanni exhaled yet another sigh of relief. He just had to keep this up until Sunday night when it would be too late to complete the assignment. Cameras were due back Monday morning by 9AM.

Fourteen episodes of FIFA 19 and two bowls of chicken soup later Giovanni sat fully-dressed, wide-awake and staring into the darkness. He could not get the assignment out of his mind. Turning on the lamp once more and reaching into the book bag carelessly tossed under the bed he took out the digital camera and project instructions. He read through the examples. All of them  this time. All of the suggestions for normal activities that all normal kids and families do. A single silent tear slipped silently down his cheek. Then another. And soon he was crying all of the tears he had held inside for all of the memories he had never been able to make.

Kyle had been born when he was four. Too young for Giovanni to really have any lasting memories. That first year had been pretty normal. Well fairly uneventful. But without warning everything changed. At fourteen months Kyle appeared to have missed all the milestones for a kid his age. He didn't reach for food, he seemed to hate everything, he wasn't trying to walk and he hadn't tried to talk. Not one word.

His dad became depressed. His mom became obsessed. And Giovanni became invisible. He walked. He talked. He excelled at everything. And absolutely no one seemed to care.

For a while he tried harder. He thought maybe if he could do better - be better, his parents would notice. Notice him. But they didn't. They were too busy working with Kyle. Helping Kyle to become the son they already had in Giovanni. But, apparently, one was not enough... never going to be enough. All the attention was focused on Kyle and Giovanni was left to fend for himself.

It wasn't on purpose or even planned. It wasn't malicious. It wasn't even what his parents wanted. They would never love him any less. They would never want him to be hurt. But they were so caught up in their own pain they couldn't see any of his. And not wanting to add any more to their seemingly never-ending burdens Giovanni never said a word.

But he was a kid. And he couldn't help how he acted sometimes. And sometimes his hurt came out in ways he could not yet control. Like his smart mouth and his wise cracks. He wanted to make friends but was afraid to. What if they wanted to come over and saw how things were at his house?

He wanted to play on a team or belong to a group. But what if they wanted his dad to take a turn at being a coach? Or what if it was his mother's turn to be the snack bearer or den mother or anything where she'd have to bring Kyle along? What if he completed his project and showed everyone his bio and they saw that in his home he didn't even exist? At least not now. When was it ever going to be his turn?

The softness of the tapping at the door let him know it was his mom. Probably bringing him yet another popsicle or a snack. But when he opened the door and saw his father standing there he was confused. His dad never came to his room.

"Is… Is something wrong dad? Did I do something wrong?"

"No son. Why would you ask that?"

"Well, is everything okay with Kyle?"

"Yes Gio, everything is fine. Your mother told me that you weren't feeling well so I came to see if you were alright. If there was anything that I could do to make you feel better."

Giovanni didn't know how to answer. *Who was the strange man standing at his door?*

"Look son," his dad began cautiously, "I know we don't spend much time together and I know you don't have much time for me. But maybe since you're still awake we could watch a movie together or maybe you could teach me how to play one of those video games you love so much."

Giovanni's mind was racing.

How could his father think he didn't have time for him?

He wanted to reassure his dad that he loved him. He wanted to jump in his father's arms and wrap himself into a little ball in his lap. The way he used to do when he was little. He remembered.

He remembered how safe and loved and happy he'd felt sitting on his daddy's lap resting his head against the firm chest and hearing the beating of his heart. He wanted to be daddy's little boy again. But he couldn't. The pain just wouldn't let him let go.

So instead he did what Giovanni does. Curtly he turned to his father and said, "Why don't you just go ahead and play with Kyle that's what you really want to do anyway. That's all you ever want to do."

Now it was his father's turn to be speechless. And confused. He couldn't believe what he was hearing. Did Giovanni think he would rather be with Kyle? Was it true?

Taken aback by the accusation and not knowing what else to say his father left the room. Giovanni was not surprised. He knew his father wanted to be with Kyle and he knew that's where he was going.

Heartbroken and disgusted at the same time Giovanni took solace in the big beanbag chair and curled up pretending that it was his father's lap and hating that he wanted it to be so.

He wasn't sure how long he slept but when he looked up his parents were there. Both of them. Standing silently together looking down at him. And then his mother began to cry.

His father spoke first. His words soft and filled with emotion. He tried to tell Giovanni how much they loved him. How proud they were of him. And how sorry they were that they had not been the parents he needed.

His mother talked about how independent he had become when Kyle was just a baby and how much he seemed to be able to do on his own. Rather than hold him back they had just let him grow and develop and excel. He seemed to have wanted it that way and so they backed off and turned their attention to Kyle who was much more in need of their attention and time.

They realized now that this was a mistake. That even though he seemed so capable of doing everything on his own he was still just a little boy and he still needed his mommy and daddy to be just that. His father asked for his forgiveness. His mother asked for his love. And at that moment Giovanni knew that his project would be the best in the class once again. But this time for all the right reasons.

WORKSHEET #7

1. Have you ever felt abandoned by your parent(s) at a time when you needed them to be there just for you?

   _____

   _____

   _____

2. Do you sometimes feel they give too much attention to your sibling(s) and not enough to you? _____

   If so, have you ever talked to them about it? _____

   How did that go? Did your parent(s) make a change? If not, why not?

   _____

   _____

   _____

3. Do you like being independent or wish you had more help?

   _____

   _____

   _____

   _____

4. Do your parents show you the same amount or kind of love they show to your sibling? If not, how do you wish it was different?

_____

_____

_____

_____

5. Have you had situations arise at school that made you feel embarrassed for your family or situation? What happened?

_____

_____

_____

_____

_____

6. Do your feelings about your sibling cause you to behave differently in different situations?

_____

_____

_____

Just an Ordinary Girl

Abigail Reynolds was an ordinary girl in absolutely every ordinary way. Except one. No it wasn't her bouncy red curls or the way her big beautiful brown eyes reminded you of Bambi. It wasn't her slim athletic form, her perfect smile or the masterly way she played video games like a virtuoso even when she had never seen or played the game before. It wasn't even the quaint little house her family lived in right next door to Grandma Kate. Abigail Reynolds led a perfectly normal life. There was nothing special about her. Except her name. No, not Reynolds. It's a perfectly common American name. Absolutely ordinary... but her first name... now that was something extraordinary.

From the day she was born her family called her Abbygail. You know,

like two names. Abby and Gail. That was the only name she knew. Abigail spent her entire life correcting every teacher she'd ever had and every stranger she'd ever met. She didn't have a nickname like some of the other kids. And she didn't want one. She refused to be called just Abby. Abby gail was just fine.

Everyone eventually got the hang of it and as the years went by even her name became ordinary to absolutely everyone she knew. Everyone except Thatcher, the youngest of the Reynold clan. But that was no surprise to anyone. Not even Abigail because as ordinary as she had become... Thatcher was the exact opposite. There was absolutely nothing ordinary about him.

Thatcher had thick black straight hair that was determined to mimic a porcupine on full alert. His body seemed crooked where it should have been straight. He never smiled, never played, never did any of the things ordinary kids like Abigail did. He didn't watch TV or jump in the mud. He didn't even talk. Thatcher was as unordinary as a kid could get. But in the Reynold's house... even this was ordinary.

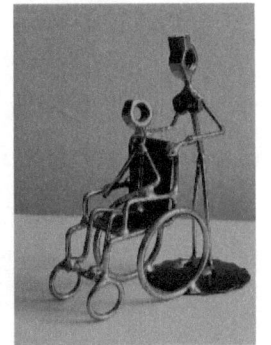

Abigail loved her strange little brother. His quirkiness reminded her of the oddity or her name. Sometimes she forgot how different he was. Sometimes she forgot about him. But sometimes... she tried to make memories.

In autumn dad would sit Thatcher in the middle of the front yard while they raked the brightly colored leaves into a huge pile right beside his chair. When the pile was almost as tall as she was Abigail would jump into it tossing the brilliant vibrant crunchiness into the air. Showering her little brother with multicolored rain.

In the winter she would have mom wrap him in a blanket and sit him on the front porch so he could watch them build a snowman. Abigail would always take some of the snow and sit directly in front of Thatcher. She would lay his palm on hers, so he could feel the gelid velvet always being careful to take his hand away and replace his fuzzy mitten before his fingers got too cold.

In the spring they would lay together on a blanket in the yard and stare at the sky as Abigail pointed to the various clouds with funny shapes and gave them magical names.

One evening as they lay there it began to rain. A soft gentle warm coming-of-summer rain. Abigail jumped up to dance in the tiny sparkling drops. Her face glistening as the radiant sun shone despite heaven's tears and Thatcher for the first time in quite a while through the haze like mist touching his upturned face gurgled his laughter and smiled with his eyes.

Abigail like most ordinary teenage girls loved to dance. She would download her favorite music on her phone, close her door and become the megastar of her dreams.

It was during one of these ordinary moments that something extraordinary began to happen.

• • •

Abigail's parents had been invited to a wedding. Usually Grandma Kate came over to watch Thatcher, but this was a cousin's wedding and Abigail knew her grandma wanted to go too. So, as she sometimes does Abigail offered to look after Thatcher so all the grownups could go.

They watched some TV then Thatcher watched his sister slay video games. Later, Abigail fed him his favorite - a bowl of cream of rice with unsalted butter. When the meal was done Abigail did what ordinary girls do. She turned on her music and started to dance.

Thatcher watched uninterestedly at her slender form flinging and flailing around the room. Then in the midst of this very ordinary moment something extraordinary happened. Abigail begin to sing. No, she wasn't an exceptionally gifted vocalist. In fact her voice, like practically everything else about her was pretty ordinary. But it was pretty. And pleasant. And passionate. For Thatcher it was pure magic. His eyes began to dance. The music and the words were hypnotic.

Abigail was so caught up in her own diva dazzle that she almost missed the moment. She twirled well tripped actually into the sunlight hitting the edge of the wall mirror just right so that as she spun past she saw the excitement in Thatcher's eyes. His mouth open. She gasped lost her balance and fell quite ungracefully to the thankfully soft padding of the carpet below.

She ran crawled to where Thatcher sat. Their eyes locked for the first time she could remember. She stared at him. Afraid to move. Afraid to mess up the magical moment. She inhaled softly and began to sing. Again. Thatcher grateful for another moment of joy tried again to sing along. It was the most ordinary thing he had ever done and there was nothing ordinary about it.

Mother's Day was only a few weeks away, so Abigail did what any ordinary girl would do. She came up with the perfect gift to surprise their mom. She would help Thatcher learn to sing.

It was almost comical how hard Abigail went out of her way to make sure that no music was played anywhere near her little brother. She didn't want anything to ruin the moment and spoil her special surprise.

She even offered to ride along to his doctor's appointment then feigned a headache asking the radio be turned off which earned her a look-see by an overly concerned nurse. But after Abigail confided her plan; the nurse, thrilled with the possibility of Thatcher's progress asked mom "to keep the radio off on the ride back home so Abigail's brain could rest."

The week before Mother's Day was unusually warm. Abigail like most ordinary girls convinced her dad to take the cover off the pool and fill it almost a month earlier than planned. The next day Abigail shivered as she slipped into the icy water.

It would be days before the warmth of the sun caught up with the heater bringing the pool to a comfortable state. But Abigail couldn't wait. She wanted to work with Thatcher - but she also wanted to swim.

Abigail remembered how much her little brother loved the cold feel of the snow on his palm. With a little coaxing she convinced mom to help sit Thatcher on the edge of the pool so his feet and ankles were submerged with the promise to take him out before he got too cold. Mom agreed and drove off to get items from the nearby grocery.

Abigail dove into the icy water popping up just in front of where Thatcher sat. He watched her. Waiting. She did not disappoint.

After several tries she had found the song that clearly was his favorite and there, alone in the pool, they begin to sing. At first it was garbled. Just a word. But in minutes Thatcher's mind was at work and he sang an entire line. *Hallelujah!* Abigail was so excited that she paddled around in a circle then jumped up to hug him.

Startled, Thatcher lost his balance and began slipping into the icy water.

"No!" she shouted, this couldn't be happening. She couldn't hold on. Just as he would surely have slipped under dad's strong hand came out of nowhere steadying him safely back onto the side.

"Abby! What were you thinking?" asked Dad.

His voice was firm but filled with compassion. Shaken by the turn of events and knowing all too well what could have happened Abigail just stared blankly unable to respond. Then, remembering her mission and the need for surprise she responded as any other ordinary teenage girl would do.

"Dad" she retorted, "my name is Abigail. Not Abby." Then, seeing the hurt in her father's eyes she added "I'm sorry. I just wanted him to have some fun. I promise I'll be more careful."

Relieved and pleased at the time she was spending with Thatcher dad retreated to his mother's house next-door where the undeniable smell of freshly baking brownies was wafting out across the yard. Abigail was relieved too. She started to think what could have happened if her father had not come along when he did. She looked apologetically at Thatcher and noticed he was shivering a little too.

One last dip and she would take them both in the house. Grandma's brownies always tasted as good as they smelled. She thought to herself how happy everyone would be on Sunday when Thatcher gave mom the best present ever.

She began to sing their song one last time as she smiled at Thatcher, twirled and fell into the water striking her head on the concrete edge and slipping into unconsciousness and she sank. Thatcher waited a moment for her to pop up, anxious to have his turn. But she never came.

Confused. Or not. Thatcher began to sing his line. And he sang it over and over again and again getting louder with every turn. All the grownups appeared in the yard at the same moment. Dad's brownie hit the ground as mom struggled to hold onto her shopping bag. Thatcher was singing and Abigail was drowning. Grandma screamed. Mom dialed and Dad dove. They did exactly what any ordinary grownups would do.

On Sunday morning when most ordinary families were in church Abigail's were at the hospital to take her home. Kneeling in front of his chair Abigail thanked her little brother for ruining her surprise. She knew he probably didn't understand and she didn't care. She was that grateful.

Softly she started singing their song and right on cue, as if nothing else out of the ordinary had happened, Thatcher joined her singing his line.

Wrapping her arms around him she whispered, "Happy Mother's Day from both of us." And her mother, now understanding Abigail's role in Thatcher's miracle burst into tears and hugged them both.

"I love you Abigail" she cried.

"Abby" Thatcher echoed.

And for the first time Abigail heard her name with her heart instead of her ears and thought just Abby was the most ordinarily beautiful name in the world.

WORKSHEET #8

1. What has your sibling done in the past that surprised you?

    _____

    _____

    _____

    _____

2. Does your sibling sing? _____

    Do they enjoy music? _____

    How do you know? _____

    _____

    _____

3. What kinds of things do you enjoy doing with your sibling?

    _____

    _____

    _____

    _____

    _____

    _____

4. What things do you do with your sibling that you don't enjoy?

_____

_____

_____

_____

_____

5. What things do you wish you could do with your sibling that they are not able to do?

_____

_____

_____

_____

_____

6. Does your family know how you feel?

_____

_____

_____

_____

_____

The Other Brother

"Robert, Robert Cheatham! Are you sleeping in my class again? Wake up!"

Robbie sat bolt upright in his chair knocking the open science book he'd been using as a pillow off his desk in the process. Fumbling to hurriedly pick up the massive text he somehow managed to fall sideways through the open space onto the floor. Unfortunately, it was one of those one-piece student desks with the bar slanted upward from the seat to the desktop and of course he'd also managed to get his leg so twisted he was momentarily stuck and couldn't figure out how to get up or down.

The chuckles, snorts and giggles his classmates had been attempting to stifle erupted into peels of raucous laughter. Robbie looked up just in time to see Stuart Dennison with a cellphone in his hand blatantly recording the entire shameful incident. He wanted to protest being live streamed to the masses of the outside world but a pair of red leather boots and a long green tent of a skirt reminiscent of a rejected Christmas elf stepped right into the path of the feed.

"Robert, if this is your attempt at being the class clown congratulations, mission accomplished. But if this is your attempt at being dismissed so you don't have to take this morning's test you are sadly mistaken, young man."

"Wait, said a snarky voice, "he's not getting sent to the office after a stunt like that?"

Robbie cringed. He couldn't bear the thought of creating another problem for his mom. She had her hands full enough already,

"I'm sorry Mrs. Bellum," Robert spoke softly - clearly embarrassed.

"It wasn't on purpose, I promise."

"He promised!" mocked Stuart and the whole class erupted into a new wave of laughs.

Robbie felt the redness creep up his neck and flood his face as he fought back the tears that would surely get him labeled soft or even worse a punk. Mrs. Bellum must have seen his struggle. She turned around blocking his face from the unmerciful lens and ordered Stuart to turn off the phone before she became its new owner. Then, being a true teacher, she ordered "Robert into the hallway" for a private discussion on his actions.

Stumbling he awkwardly rose from the floor and bolted out the door into the privacy of the vacant hallway. Placing his hands on his knees he gulped in the fresh air grateful to be away from the prying eyes of his middle school jury. After what seemed an eternity he heard the class quiet down and begin the final ten-minute study period Mrs. Bellum allows before each test begins.

He heard the soft click of the door and looked up to see the concerned face of his teacher staring down at him. He gulped again underestimating the psychic powers of discernment all great teachers possess. Gently placing a hand on his arm, she queried,

"Do you want to talk about it?"

Robbie was shocked. He expected to get a handed a pink slip to the dean or at least yelled at for causing such an uproar. Slowly letting out his breath he admitted that things had been pretty rough at home lately. They recently had to move to a smaller apartment and he was supposed to share a room with his twin brother, but that wasn't going well at all.

Mrs. Bellum was taken aback. She didn't even know Robbie had a brother. She was sure he didn't attend Marshall even though it was the only middle school in the district. Keeping her voice level, she asked Robbie if he felt rested enough to take the test. He hesitated, he hadn't studied at all last night. In fact, he'd barely been able to study at all for the past week.

Calmly Mrs. Bellum wrote out a pink slip and told him he could take the test when he returned on Monday. She handed him the paper atop his science book and returned to the class who, seeing that Robbie was not returning with her, erupted into laughter again. *Great. Now mom's going to be even more stressed.*

Robbie thought dreading the call the dean was soon to make. But when he looked at the pass he had to reread it to make sure it said what it did.

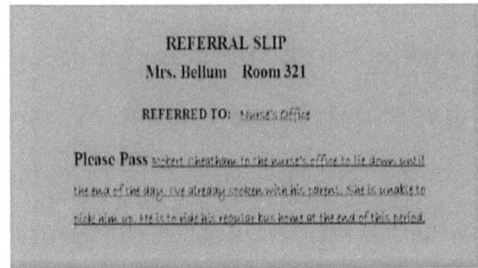

"Please pass Robert Cheatham to the nurse's office to lie down until the end of the day. I've already spoken with his parent. She is unable to pick him up. He is to ride his regular bus home at the end of this period."

It was as if the weight of the world lifted off his shoulders. Mrs. Bellum was an angel. She'd let the other students think he was being sent to detention. Or worse. She'd helped him save face. Students can be cruel. Especially pre-pubescent pre-teens jockeying for position in the hierarchy of social standing in this town's only capital of middle school madness. In a world full of labels, she'd saved him. He headed to the nurse's office for what was going to be the best seventy-five minutes of sleep he'd had in days.

On Monday morning Robert showed up at Mrs. Bellum's door instead of reporting to his homeroom/activity period. Completing his test in record time he proudly handed over his paper. Mrs. Bellum smiled broadly. She quickly graded the exam placing a "B+" at the top of the page. But instead of handing it over to Robbie she asked him to sit down.

She spoke softly without meeting his eyes. She told him she'd done some checking over the weekend. Robbie's heart sank. She knew. But she didn't say what he thought she would. She did tell him that she'd learned he had a brother, Daniel who attended a special day program for special kids just a few blocks from their new apartment. That his mother worked very hard to provide a loving home for them both but had to take on extra-hours at her job leaving Robbie to look after his brother most evenings until she could get home.

Mrs. Bellum told Robbie she was proud of him for taking on so much responsibility but was worried about how much it was interfering with his studies... and his sleep. She offered to meet with his mom to discuss the situation.

Robbie was mortified. The last thing he wanted was to make his mom feel worse. He knew how bad she felt about him having to watch Danny already. Things had been really tough for Danny since he was born. Robbie was in perfect health, but Danny had been sickly since day one. He'd had all kinds of respiratory problems as a baby 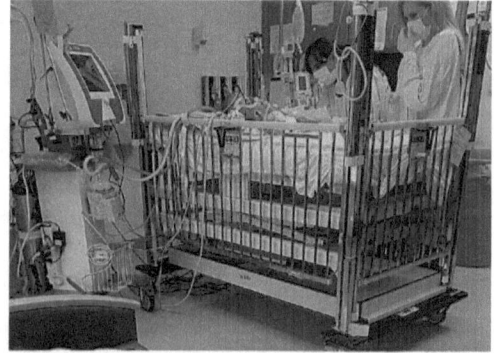 and was in and out of the hospital for months at a time. They had even moved to his mother's hometown, so they could have help with Danny.

But things got tough again after grandma died last year. She had lived with them and been Danny's caretaker when mom was away from home. And now she was gone and they'd moved here and everything had changed.

Robbie heard himself telling Mrs. Bellum everything. He didn't want to... it just kind of started spilling out; a simple admission or two at a time but then it just poured.

Mrs. Bellum was wonderful. She just listened. And when he was spent Robbie knew that she was a way to help his mom get what she needed to make life more bearable for everybody. Mrs. Bellum promised she wouldn't phone until that evening after his mom had gotten home.

It was a relief to know that Danny would have better care too. He was such a great kid. Just a little difficult to understand. They may look exactly alike but he and his brother couldn't be more different. Sometimes Danny would cry for hours and sometimes he would laugh out loud for no apparent reason. Some days he would eat boiled potatoes for every meal and other days he barely ate at all.

Losing grandma and now having to move to a new place had been hard on all of them but it was hardest for Danny. He never handled surprises well. Not even good ones. And now his whole life had changed. Heck... his whole world.

Mama called it "Too much, too soon."

His coping skills just weren't mature enough to handle this many life changes at once. He wanted his old life back. He was familiar and comfortable with that routine and now to make things even worse he'd had to start a new school with strange teachers. He tried to keep it together at school but when he got home he would melt down or shut down from working so hard all day just to cope. That's what a lot of special kids do. They try to live up to everyone's expectations when they're someplace else. Then, when they get to their safe place all the anxiety and stress rushes out to release itself any way it can. And it's usually not very pretty.

Mama used to be waiting at the bus stop for Danny with open arms. They would walk in through the door holding hands like little kids. Then Danny would lean his forehead into mom's, and he would close his eyes and let out a giant sigh. They would stand there like that for what seemed an eternity.

Sometimes he would lay his head on mom's shoulder and on really bad days he would pull her to the couch curling up on the soft cushions with his head in her lap like he was still a little kid.

But on really really bad days he would just walk past us. Yes. Even her. Slipping straight from the bus into the sanctity and quiet of his dark room closing the door shutting out the presence of anything or anyone until he was ready to rejoin the world.

Now this is where it gets messy cause mom doesn't meet him at the bus anymore. I do. And the only room he has to go to is the one we share.

I've been careful though not to let mom see just how hard this has been on me. I love Danny. He's my brother. But he's so moody and unpredictable. Sometimes I get mad at him. Sometimes I get tired of being responsible for him.

And sometimes – when he's really stressed out, I'm really afraid of him. Not just of what he'll do to me... but of what he'll do to himself. I never know if his medication is working for him or against him.

Mom had weaned him completely off and he was turning into a fairly nice kid, then the director at the new center told mom all the kids have to take their meds every day to enhance their behavior modification strategies. But Danny has a lot of sensitivities to certain foods and additives. The same medication that calms him down on Monday can make him hallucinate on Tuesday and downright mean on Wednesday and, well, you get the picture.

It's like living on a roller coaster with a slow climb to the top and a drop that takes your breath away over and over again.

I see him trying. I hear her crying. And inside I feel like all of us are dying just a little every day from the misery and pressures of how our lives have become.

Mrs. Bellum is the closest thing we've ever had to a miracle. If she knows people and ways to get Danny more of the help he needs... I'm all for it. And I know that even though she might be a little embarrassed at first – mom will appreciate it too.

Mrs. Bellum is one of the nicest ladies I know. She's been teaching for like forever. I believe she knows what she's doing. I'm pretty sure it will really help us. All of us.

WORKSHEET #9

1. Have you ever confided in a teacher or counselor at your school?
    If yes, did it help talk about your sibling? If no, would you ever?

    _____

    _____

2. Has living with a special needs child made your life more difficult
    than you imagine it would be if your sibling was NT?

    _____

    _____

    _____

3. Do you sometimes feel you have to hide your family situation or
    things about your sibling from other students?

    _____

    _____

4. Do you think all kids have things in their life they don't want to
    share? _____What about you?_____

    _____

    _____

When All You Want Is Time

"Mom… mom… Mom? Do you have a minute?"

"Sure, honey. Just give me a few more seconds to finish up with your brother.

You know how important it is that we maintain consistency in his routine."

"Yes, of course, mom. I know."

And she did know.

Schedules and routines were a way of life in the Rivera household. If you ever wanted to know what time it was all you had to do was look and see what Joey was doing and you could pretty much set your watch by it. Right now her mother was sitting putting pressure on selected positions of the weighted blanket that Joey liked to be covered with when he took his nap. Angel looked again and saw her mom pressing ever so gently on his shoulders. Yep. 2:15.

Knowing that this was not going to end by the time she needed her answer Angel slipped back outside the bedroom door, grabbed her jacket and quietly headed down the stairs. If she didn't start walking now, she would be late. She was used to it. Mom had forgotten again. Once outside she pulled her jacket tightly around her own shoulders, tucked her head and bravely began walking into the wind.

● ● ●

The skies were dark and ominous and already Angel was regretting her decision praying that it didn't rain before she got to class. She began to run feeling free and happy for the first time that day.

She loved ballet. It was her escape. The one place she could go and not have to worry about what Joey was doing. After class Angel stepped out onto the wet pavement. It had drizzled while she was inside, but it seemed to have come to an end. She was deciding whether or not to phone home for a ride when a cheery voice called out to her -

"Angel! Angelina Rivera? We're going out for ice cream and orange juice smoothies. My mom said she'll take you home after. Come on!"

It was a miracle. Things like this just didn't happen to her every day. Belinda was a godsend. This invitation could not have come at a better time. Ben and Jerry's was only a few blocks away in the Bakersville Food Court and she knew she'd be home long before dark so happily she ran to the car and joined her smiling friend.

Belinda's mom sat and giggled with the girls as they took long licks from the cookie dough ice cream filled cones. They'd had samples - in fact they'd sampled every single flavor in the place before all deciding that today's special Flavor-of-the-Day was in fact the most delicious.

And long after the cones were gone, they were still there now. Only now they were sipping smoothies with real fruit inside. Laughing, talking and sharing funny stories. Angel didn't tell any stories about her family. Instead she listened intently to the ones Belinda shared and laughed and sighed at all the right places wishing she had stories like that to tell too.

"Uhm... sorry, Mrs. Bradford," was all Angel could embarrassedly manage to murmur under her breath as the once joyful pair departed the doorway and eased down the front stairs.

Next time I'll be sure to call my mom she added silently hoping that there would be a next time. Mara Lina Rivera was a sweet lady but when she was mad she was a force to be reckoned with.

And Angel, losing track of the time had been cloaked in darkness as she opened her front door with the Bradfords close behind. A little too close apparently as Angel was sure Belinda's acquiescing mother's eyelashes were singed by the fiery tone her own mother had spat out.

"Mom, did you have to be so mean to them?" Angel queried cautiously. "They were just being nice to me and we had such a good time."

"You may have been having a good time, mi hija but I was worried sick about you."

"I'm sorry...." Angel's voice trailed off, "I just forgot to call."

"You forgot to call?" Mara Lina snapped.

"Oh, Dios mio! How could you not remember?"

"I went to ballet mom. Did you remember to take me? I told you practice was going to start an hour earlier this week because of the recital coming up. You said you wouldn't forget, but you did. Like you always do."

Angel looked down at the floor below, "You never remember about me."

Angel's words though softly spoken struck her mother with the sting of a cold towel wielded unmercifully on a hot summer day. It was true. She had forgotten about Angel. Again.

"Oh Chica, lo siento mucho. I'm so sorry. How was practice? Where did you go after? Did you have a good time?"

Angel could hear the remorse in her mother's quivering tone. She saw the distraught helplessness in her mother's eyes. Angel was not trying to be mean. But she was hurt too. Her mother never seemed to have time for her anymore. In fact, Angel could not recall the last time she had her mother's full attention. Or her time. Not to herself... Angel's mind had drifted. *What was her mother saying?*

"Yes Gabriella, I'm so sorry if I seemed rude. Thank you for taking Angelina   out with you. Please tell Belinda that next time it's my treat. Yes... that would   be wonderful. Belinda is such a sweet girl. And so talented. I can't wait to see her in the recital. She's going to be famous someday. Yes... yes... Goodbye."

And with the click on the other end of the phone Angel's heart melted. She loved her mother so much and the effusive praise for Belinda's mediocre talent was such a grand gesture. Her mother had gone out of her way to smooth things over and Angelina was truly grateful.

"Thank you mommie," she murmured burying her face in her mother's soft curls, "Thank you for fixing it with the Bradfords."

"So," her mother asked cheerfully pulling her into a warm and playful embrace,

"What did you ladies do?"

"We had ice cream and smoothies and we talked about our families for hours!" Angel felt her mother stiffen. The arm around her shoulder suddenly felt like a lead weight.

"Well, they talked, and I just listened but it was fun. They do so many things together. You know, just the two of them. Real mother - daughter stuff."

"Like what?" her mother asked quietly.

"Hair, nails, $5 Tuesdays at the movies. And ice cream. Lots and lots of ice cream!"

"Oh," Mara Lina said turning away, "Ya veo."

"And mom they talk. They really really talk. And her mom... she really listens." Angel finished. Her own voice barely a whisper.

"Girl talk," Mara Lina said with a smile. "Charla de chicas. We need that. Just you and me. ¿Solo nosotros, Si?"

But before she could answer there was Joey. Rushing into the moment in some kind of crisis. Probably night terrors. He often woke up screaming and crying from the schizophrenic like hallucinations everyone believed were from the new meds he was taking.

"Mom, you really need to help him right now. He's so scared" said Angelina surprising herself with her genuine concern for her little brother's needs.

"Are you sure? What about our girl talk?"

"Maybe tomorrow - after practice if daddy can stay with Joey. He's coming back from his business trip in the morning. He always comes to visit when he gets back. Maybe we can take Gabriella and her mom for ice cream."

"Ice cream?" Joey asked. "Please Angel. Can I have some ice cream too?"

"Okay." Angel smiled hugging her little brother for the first time in a while. "Tomorrow let's have family day and we'll all go out for ice cream together. We can invite the Bradfords next time."

"Angelina," her mother whispered, squeezing her hand, "Gracias. Thank you. I love you, mi hija... and I'm sorry."

"Te amo. I love you too mommie. It's okay. We'll have time." said Angel believing every word she spoke.

It really was all she'd ever wanted and now she knew her mother wanted that too. They would make time. Somehow. Maybe not all the time. But for now... some time would be enough.

WORKSHEET #10

1. Has your parent ever missed something that was important to you? If so, was it because of your sibling or something else?

   _____

   _____

2. Does having a special needs child in your home cause problems with managing everyone else's time or does your family have a great system?

   _____

   _____

   _____

   _____

3. Does your sibling participate in any extra-curricular activities?

   _____

4. Have you been able to do things you've wanted to: teams, classes, parties, accept invitations, hang out with friends?

   _____

   _____

Let Him Ride

A substitute in your classroom is one thing. But a substitute driving your bus. Now that is something else...

Usually all little kids like winter but this year the weather sucked. Today was no exception. At 6:53 a.m. it was still pretty dark outside. Frigid at only 23 degrees, the roads were icy, and traffic was already moving slower than usual. Under normal circumstances this may have been just another routine morning on Bus 55, but the new driver had already missed two stops and had to go back to pick up kids whose parents were upset that they'd had to wait. One of those dads had missed his ride to work and given the sub driver an earful. Her day had started out badly and quickly moved to worse. And of all the days to be absent Alice Parker was home sick. That in itself should not have been a big deal but today well... today, it kinda was.

Her: Move over and let this young lady sit down.
Him: No.
Girl: Move so I can sit down.
Him: No.
Girl: I'm cold. It's warmer up here. Move.
Him: I already told you no.
Her: Maybe you can sit by the window.

(silence)

Her: Can you let her past you, please?

Him: No.

Girl: I don't want to sit by the window. I'm cold.

Boy: Can't you make him move. You're the driver.

Her: Little boy, you can sit anywhere else on the bus.

Boy: Yea. Move.

Her: May she please sit here.

Him: No. You're making me angry.

Her: Well you need to calm down.

Boy: Yea. Calm down freak!

Her: And if I don't get moving we're going to be late.

Him: Too bad! That's not my problem! Now leave me alone!

Girl: Oh my gosh, Manny. (pushing him) Just move over already.

Him: No! I am not moving and you can't make me! He shouted as he turned in his seat shoving the demanding little girl to the floor of the bus. She cried. He cussed. And of course, a scuffle ensued between him and her. No. Not Sarah Anne. The sub lady. The driver. There was literally a fight between Him and Her.

Driving a school bus full of feisty little overzealous school kids at the crack of dawn in the dead of winter is generally an ordeal by itself. But being a substitute driver on the first day with an unfamiliar route the morning after an ice storm was bound to become an epic fail. Epic.

The poor lady was so frazzled she quit. One day on the job and she was gone. One encounter with Manny Parker was all it took. She never even made it to the school. She used her cellphone to call dispatch and stood outside the open door in the freezing cold. The minute the replacement driver showed up and began walking towards the bus she jumped into a long black car that had pulled up unnoticed on the other side of the road and disappeared into the dawn. Forever. Yep. It was just one of those days.

When the bus arrived at the Newberry Preparatory Academy for Upper and Lower Grades Sara rose from her seat in the third row and ran into the building. Past her locker, past her classroom and straight into the Principal's office to tell him her side of the story. She could have taken her time because Manny Parker was in no hurry to get inside the school. In fact, he was the last one off the bus. As usual.

Manny's father stared straight ahead as he drove the 15 minutes to the house. It looked as if he was calculating the treacherous dangers of the icy road when in actuality he barely noticed the salt covered concrete with the intermittent patches of death.

When the door opened and Alice saw Manny walk in behind her father she quickly ended her call with Dilara and waited for the lecture that was sure to follow. Somehow someway this was going to be her fault. It usually was. Her father did not disappoint.

"If only you'd been on the bus instead of pretending to be sick" and "You just wanted to talk all day on the phone - is Dilara skipping too?"

He even threw out a "that's probably why your mother left" which hit its mark causing Alice to dissolve into silent stinging tears and escape defeated into her room.

Everything her father knew about Manny's condition he learned from her. Everything her father felt about his situation he blamed on her. If something bad was happening, Alice knew it would be her responsibility to fix it and make it right.

The next morning they all piled into the car and pulled out onto the still icy road. No bus for anyone today and Manny had taken longer than usual to get ready thrown off by the schedule change. Mr. Parker was speeding, trying to make it to the school then downtown to his office before eight when he needed to clock in. When he finally pulled up in front of the main door he looked pleadingly at Alice. Alice saw his anguish and smiled.

"It's ok, dad. I'll take care of it. I'll get them to let him ride."

Principal Davies was a little surprised to see the Parker kids sitting outside his office door. He smiled at Alice and even asked her how she was feeling because he knew she'd stayed home sick the day before. Alice's maturity belied her twelve years. She was poised and somber. A little girl with an old old soul.

"My father tried to wait to speak with you, but he couldn't risk missing any more time from work. It took him over an hour to come and pick up Manny yesterday. He got a warning from his boss."

"I see." said Principle Davies absently stroking his chin with his thumb as he always did when he was thinking,

"Please. Do come in. We need to get this all figured out."

Manny followed his sister into the office as Principal Davies softly closed the door behind them.

He remembered how sensitive Manny was to loud noises and didn't want to trigger an elopement or a meltdown. Manny had an IEP meeting a few weeks ago and all of the staff had worked together to create a great plan for him when he was at school but failed to realize the struggles he and his sister endured every day to get him there.

Some kids can be mean. Cruel actually. They take great pleasure in criticizing the differences and difficulties other children face. They are hateful and hurtful. Especially to special needs kids who look or act differently.

Bullying exists almost everywhere but for kids that don't think or act as quickly as others it's a daily nightmare. Manny was a sweet kid who wanted to please his teachers, but his OCD made him unwavering in assigned behaviors.

What??? Alice tried to focus on what Mr. Davies was saying, it was something about "suspending Manny from the bus" ...That would be the worst possible thing that could happen for all of them. Either she would have to stay home and supervise Manny because he couldn't be left in the house alone or their father would end up losing his job trying to transport them to school each day.

"Principal Davies you can't!" She heard herself saying, "Please, let him ride. You don't know how terrible it's been for us... I mean him..." her voice trailed off but not before something in her tone caught both Mr. Davies' attention and Manny's.

"I'm sorry," said Manny sadly to his sister, "I try to be good, to ignore them, but they're just so mean. And they say such bad things about me. I just want to be left alone. I didn't mean to hurt Sara but she touched me without asking... Maybe I should stay home."

"Oh, Manny. It's not your fault. Not yesterday. Not ever. You were just following directions and doing what Mrs. Franklin told you to do."

Principal Davies was intrigued. *Following directions? Surely his regular driver hadn't told him to push Sara Ann or argue with an adult driver. And Sara Ann had touched him first? And where was the driver anyway?*

"But they're so mean to you Alice," Manny's voice was trembling almost as much as he was, but he had to protect his sister.

He gathered his courage and continued,

"Everybody wants to fight you because you make them leave me alone. Last week, when you told Elijah to stop calling me a freak, he said he was going to get you if he caught you by yourself. I don't want him to get you Alice. I don't want him to hurt you like he does when he hits me."

"Whoa there," interrupted Principal Davies, "Someone's been hitting you and threatening your sister?" His voice became even more concerned.

"Who hurt you Manny? Who's been calling you names?

And what did Mrs. Franklin tell you to do?"

"Uhm..." Manny's voice cracked, and he looked like he was about to cry.

Alice knew Principal Davies meant well but she also knew how Manny would react if he was afraid or became confused by being asked too many questions at once...

She had to explain –

"Mrs. Franklin knew that she was going to be out of town for a week. She told us. She told all of us. She also told Manny that he was to sit in the seat right behind the substitute on the side by the aisle, so they could see him in the rear-view mirror. That way, whoever was driving could see if anybody tried to mess with Manny. I ride the bus too, but I like to sit in the back with the older kids. Well, I woke up feeling nauseous with bad stomach cramps yesterday, so my dad let me stay home. I forgot Mrs. Franklin wouldn't be there this week or I would never have let Manny ride by himself. The other kids mock him and make fun of him all the time. At his old school he had a bus monitor who rode with him but now that we're at the same school I thought I should help him. I'm his big sister... I'm supposed to protect him. And I don't mind. Really I don't... I just didn't know it would be every day."

Principal Davies stroked his chin. He was quiet. The bell rang.

Nobody moved.

"I'm going to be late," Manny said worriedly. "I don't want to be late."

"Manny," Principal Davies sounded sincere, "I'm sorry that the other students have been bullying you and your sister. I know how good you are about following directions and not breaking the rules. I now understand what happened on the bus. You didn't want to slide over because Mrs. Franklin had assigned you to that seat and you didn't want to break her trust. The other students knew that too and they were wrong to try to make you move and to call you names. I believe that you are sorry that you pushed Sara Ann. And I know you didn't mean to have an altercation with the driver. You are always very respectful of adults."

He paused, again stroking his chin, deciding what to say next.

"You were already sent home for the day yesterday and you were suspended from riding the bus this morning. I think you've been punished enough for your part in the mishap. Now I need to address those students who've been bullying you and your sister."

"Oh no," said Manny trembling even more, "If they get in trouble because of me they're going to – "

"If they get in trouble, Manny, it's because of them. Not you. They're not going to come after you or get your sister. I'll see to that. Now hurry along to class. You've got just enough time to make it. Are you okay to go by yourself?"

"Yes sir. And thank you. I didn't want my sister to get hurt."

"She won't. I promise. And I'm not going to let them hurt you anymore either."

Manny gave an awkward half smile and slipped hurriedly out of the office.

I didn't know what to say. I wasn't a snitch. But the way they treated Manny was wrong. And I was tired of almost having to fight the other kids who were constantly threatening both of us on the bus.

It was a relief to hear Mr. Davies say that he would intervene on our behalf. He was friendly and fair, but he was firm. And he was always talking about how important it was for all the students to feel safe.

I believed he would make it stop so both Manny and I could have some peace.

I breathed a sigh of relief and turning to the chair behind me picked up my bookbag and scarf from the bright shiny red leather I hadn't noticed before. I looked around the Principal's office. It was warm and pleasant and something wafting from the diffuser on the desk made the whole room smell like lavender and grape jello slime. It felt like the kind of place a kid could go to solve problems.

"Are you going to be alright?" Mr. Davies asked not sure that I was convinced he would help. "I'm certain that you haven't confided any of this to your father or he would have come to me himself."

"Well I... I..." was all I could stammer but Principal Davies knew all too well that I had not burdened my father with these truths.

"You're a very strong girl Alice but you shouldn't have to be that brave. Manny is very lucky to have you for a sister. You're his hero you know. A real champion. It takes a very special kind of person to have the compassion and the courage that you do. Your family is very blessed that you look out for Manny so well and I'm going to make sure that your father understands just how much you do to ensure that your little brother is okay. You probably think that your efforts go unnoticed. But I know. And Manny knows. And your father will know too..."

He turned to his desk and deftly filled out a small paper with a singular swipe of his pen.

"Here's a late pass from the office. It's excused. Go check on Manny and assure him that everything's okay. Then take a few minutes for yourself. I hear Dilara wants to talk to you about running for student council representative. I think the two of you would make a great pair of leaders for the rest of our student body. Now, as for the bus... Everything is going to be alright. I'm happy the situation is fixed. I'm happy - to let him ride."

WORKSHEET #11

1. Have you ever had to take up for your sibling? _____

    When you do? Do other students cause you problems?

    _____

    _____

2. Have you ever bullied someone? If yes, why? If no, why not?

    _____

    _____

    _____

3. Have you or your sibling ever been bullied? Is there one incident
    that stands out in your mind as the worst? What happened?

    _____

    _____

    _____

    _____

4. Have you confided in an adult about hurtful people?

    _____

• • •

5. Was the adult able to help you?

   If yes, how? If no, what happened?

   _____

   _____

   _____

   _____

   _____

6. What do administrators and teachers at your school need to know about what they should be doing more of to help kids that are bullied?

   _____

   _____

   _____

   _____

   _____

   _____

   _____

   _____

   _____

   _____

Have you ever wanted to write your parents or anyone else a letter about your sibling or something you have been through or your feelings about a situation? If you haven't done so already now's your chance. Go ahead. Be honest. Tell someone what you want them to know. Your thoughts are special. Your feelings are special... and your needs are special too.

_____

_____

_____

_____

_____

_____

_____

_____

_____

_____

_____

_____

_____

_____

The boy on the stairs is Marcus Booth, my ASD son

Special thanks to everyone who has traveled this journey with me to becoming a better autism mom. Hugs and prayers to everyone as we move forward in our quest to help every child feel special and loved and validated. Every child's needs are special to my heart.

Sister, Sister artwork by Maliya Elise, age 8
Haley and Rachel portrayed by Maliya Booth and Makenzie Robinson
Kathleen and Delia portrayed by Melissa Booth and Maliya Booth
Giovanni Carpenter portrayed by actor Shannon Merrill Brown